Being a
Map of the Mystery-
Marsh,
the Meadow, the Millpond & Mill &
much much more
Drawn by Erik Blegvad
1966
Road to the Airport
Stewart Peeble's
House
Mrs. Munch's
House
Road to the
Dentist's
The Lane
Elisabeth's
House

The Sea

The Mill

The Millpond

The Dancing was here

The Trap

The Marsh

The Marsh Meadow

Stewart fell out of this Willow

LEGEND

MARSH

MEADOW

TREE

HOLE

HOUSE

TELEPHONE POLES

SWAN

CYGNETS

Elisabeth and the Marsh Mystery

Elisabeth and the Marsh Mystery

by Felice Holman

illustrated by Erik Blegvad

THE MACMILLAN COMPANY, NEW YORK

COLLIER-MACMILLAN LIMITED, LONDON

This book is for
CLEMENTENE AND GIRARD WHEELER
who believe in birds and people
and know that marshes, woods,
and greensward must be preserved
for all living things.

 The Macmillan Company, New York. Collier-Macmillan Canada, Ltd., Toronto, Ontario. Library of Congress catalog card number: 66–11105. Printed in the United States of America.
FIRST PRINTING

Marshes, mysterious and wonderful, so important to the whole balance of nature, are being destroyed all around us. In my town, and perhaps in your town, marshes are being filled to create new land for building or filled just to get rid of refuse. The terrible thing is that once a marsh is gone it can never be made again. Never. Plants, animals, people, tiny creatures we cannot even see . . . bound together in a long important chain . . . all are affected, because in filling the marsh, a chain of life is broken off at its beginnings.

Saving marshes is an important work of conservationists. *Sometime, perhaps, you will be able to help raise the cry against filling our marshes. Not the least of the benefits will be that we may always be able to see and hear creatures like those Elisabeth sees and hears in this book.*

FELICE HOLMAN

THE brisk spring breeze caught Elisabeth's hair as she ran down the lane to meet her father, and she looked like a small red kite just about to leave the ground.

"Papa, Papa! Have you heard it?" she cried as her father held out his arms to keep her from blowing right past him.

"Heard what?" he asked with interest.

"The sound! The queer sound over there in the marsh!" Elisabeth gasped.

"What sort of sound?" Papa asked.

"Well," said Elisabeth, taking a deep breath and thinking hard, "you know Stewart Peebles?"

"Of course," said Papa. "Everyone around

here knows Stewart Peebles. He's ubiquitous."

Elisabeth looked sideways at Papa. "Oh, no, Stewart's all right," she said. "It's just that he's always underfoot."

"Just exactly what I said," said Papa.

"Oh," Elisabeth said thoughtfully, and she took Papa's hand, and they started up the lane.

"Well, anyway," Elisabeth continued, "you remember how Stewart always wanted to play the bugle and then how awful it sounded when he started to learn?"

"I shall never forget it," Papa said solemnly, nodding his head as he recollected.

"Well," said Elisabeth, taking another deep breath, "the sound that I heard is just like *that*."

"In the *marsh?*" asked Papa.

"Yes, way down in the back of Peebles' house."

"That makes me wonder," suggested Papa, "if what you heard could have been Stewart Peebles playing the bugle."

"In the *marsh!*" exclaimed Elisabeth.

"No better place for it," Papa said.

Elisabeth gave Papa another sideways look. "But, you see," she said, "Stewart has been wearing braces on his teeth for a long time, and he hasn't been able to blow the bugle. So it can't be that.

"It's something else," she went on. "But what?" And then she wrinkled her brow. "Or *who?*"

"What do you mean, 'or who'?" asked Papa.

"Well, I was thinking," said Elisabeth eagerly, "it could be a . . . well, a princess, for instance, being held captive by . . . oh, a wicked stepmother or something."

"There's that possibility, of course," Papa said. "But in the marsh in back of Peebles'?"

"That's just the kind of place for it," said Elisabeth with great enthusiasm.

Just then they heard other voices talking excitedly and, looking up, saw Mrs. Peebles on the porch of Mrs. Munch's house. Mrs. Peebles was making wide gestures with her hands, and Mrs. Munch was flapping her arms oddly with the elbows crooked. When they saw Elisabeth and her father, Mrs. Munch flapped right over to them, followed quickly by Mrs. Peebles.

"Did you hear it?" asked Mrs. Munch. Without waiting for an answer, she said very quickly, "I heard it over and over again, and finally I came out onto the porch with my binoculars to see if I could find out what it was. It sounded like . . ."

"Like Stewart Peebles playing the bugle?" Elisabeth rushed to ask.

"Just like that," Mrs. Munch agreed appreciatively, but Mrs. Peebles did not look quite so appreciative. In fact, she pinched her mouth up a bit.

"I looked over there to the edge of the marsh," Mrs. Munch went on, "and then, when I didn't see it, I took my binoculars away from my eyes, and *there it was!* Right in my flower bed! Not *that* far from me."

"What did you do?" asked Mrs. Peebles, unpinching her mouth.

"I screamed," said Mrs. Munch. "That's what I did. Then he raised his enormous wings" —Mrs. Munch crooked her arms as before and started to flap—"and he half flew, half ran across the garden and into the marsh."

"Ah, it's a bird, then!" said Papa, just as Elisabeth said disappointedly, "It doesn't sound a bit like a captive princess."

"A bird!" exclaimed Mrs. Peebles. "It's a monster! I saw it myself from my kitchen window."

"Oh, come now," said Papa calmly. "Try to describe it."

"Well," said Mrs. Munch quickly, before Mrs. Peebles could reply, "he was about that high," and she raised her arm up as far as she could reach.

"Shorter than that," said Mrs. Peebles.

"Taller, if anything," Mrs. Munch said, "and gray."

"Tan, I would say," said Mrs. Peebles, pinching her lips again.

"Hm," Papa mused. "This has been most interesting, ladies. I think Elisabeth and I will do a bit of investigating. Thank you so much for your help."

Elisabeth and Papa continued walking up the lane. When they looked back, Mrs. Munch had started flapping again.

"It sounds," remarked Elisabeth as they walked along the edge of the millpond, "like two different birds. Mrs. Peebles' is shorter and tan, and Mrs. Munch's is taller and gray."

"That's one of the interesting things about asking people to describe what they've seen when they're excited," said Papa. "Hardly anyone agrees, and sometimes they leave out the most important thing. Let's go home and see what we can find out about this mysterious 'monster' in our bird book."

Papa stopped walking for a minute to point out two birds that were swimming on the pond.

Elisabeth watched them with interest. "The duck in back looks like a submarine," she said. "See? His neck and head are out of the water, but the rest of him isn't."

Papa laughed. "They *are* like submarines, but they're not ducks. They're loons. They're bigger than ducks, and they swim lower in the water. Have you ever noticed the loon's funny call at night? It goes *ha-oo-oo*, *ha-oo-oo*, especially before a storm."

"I've heard it," said Elisabeth, "but I guess I thought it was really someone laughing," and she laughed, too.

As they turned away from the millpond, two swans swam into view leading six cygnets in a game of follow-the-leader. Circling around them, dipping for fish, was a black duck. There was so much to see on the millpond! Elisabeth wanted to stay and watch, but Papa said, "If we want to solve this puzzle, we're going to have to get home. Come on!"

"Now, let's see," said Papa as they entered the house and went into the study. He took the bird book down from the shelf. "What do we know about this bird?"

"Well," Elisabeth said, "he has long legs and maybe lives in the marsh."

"Right! That's enough to start on. Let's look at this page of long-legged marsh birds. Now, you see this picture of the great blue heron? . . . I would be inclined to think it was that—except for two things."

"What two things?" Elisabeth asked with interest.

"In the first place, even though the description sounds rather like the blue heron, Mrs. Munch and Mrs. Peebles must certainly know what a heron looks like, living so close to the millpond."

"And in the second place?" asked Elisabeth.

"And in the second place, no great blue heron ever sounded like a bugle. As a matter of fact, they sound rather like this," and much to Elisabeth's surprise, Papa started making a croaking sound, something like "*fronk, fronk, fronk.*"

Elisabeth had to laugh—Papa looked so serious and sounded so funny.

"And it's not any of these other long-legged birds," Papa continued, frowning. "They're egrets, and they're all white."

"What about the rest of these birds?" Elisabeth asked, pointing to the page.

"These birds are small or else just don't fit

the description at all. And these others all live in other parts of the country. I've never heard of any being seen here. No! We need help."

"But who can help us?" asked Elisabeth.

Papa thought for a minute, and then he said, "I think I will call our neighbor Mr. Thew. He works for the wildlife museum, you know, and he just might have some ideas about this."

Elisabeth waited impatiently while Papa talked and talked to Mr. Thew on the telephone. To make matters more trying, Papa kept saying tantalizing things like, "Whatever do you mean?" and "For heaven's sake!" And finally he said, "All right, Mr. Thew . . . just as soon as we've had our supper. Good-bye."

"What did he say? What did he say?" asked Elisabeth, standing on one foot in suspense.

"He says," said Papa, and he sounded puzzled, "that it could be an escaped exotic."

"An escaped exotic!" Elisabeth exclaimed. "Show me a picture of it in the book, Papa, please."

"Oh, that's not the *name* of the bird," Papa said, laughing. "The word 'exotic' means 'foreign' or 'different.' Mr. Thew thinks that this might be some strange bird, perhaps from another country, that may have escaped from somebody's private zoo. But it's a good name, and since we don't know the bird's real name,

let's call it the 'escaped exotic,' shall we? Now let's go and ask Mama to hurry our supper a bit, and then we'll be off."

"Off where?" Elisabeth asked.

"Stalking," said Papa. "We'll stalk the escaped exotic in the marsh and find out once and for all what it is. Mr. Thew is going to meet us there. After all," Papa went on, as if arguing with himself, "there are just so many things it might be. It *can't* be most of them, and it's only one of the rest of them. That kind of situation interests me. Be sure to wear your boots," he called as Elisabeth went off to dress for stalking, "and see if you can find your flashlight. It will be dark before we get home. I'm going to ask Mama for a thermos of something hot. It may get chilly."

As soon as dinner was over, Elisabeth and Papa set out. They had walked only two steps, from the kitchen door to the middle of the porch, when Papa tripped over something and said a few words under his breath that Elisabeth couldn't quite make out. Then the something sat up and said, "Hello," in a husky voice.

"Stewart!" exclaimed Elisabeth. "What are you doing?"

"Waiting for you to come and hunt for it. I knew you would."

"Oh, you are clever, Stewart!" Stewart grinned with pleasure, the bright silver braces on his teeth gleaming and flashing. Elisabeth secretly thought the braces were very elegant and dressy looking.

Then Stewart sprang to his feet, with a rather showy leap, and addressed them as if they were a considerably larger group than they were. "Now, here's my plan. We beat the bush. We section off the marsh, see, and you two start beating toward me. Have you brought any drums or anything?"

Elisabeth shook her head. Papa seemed to be

growling a little. Stewart went on, "Well, anyway, when I see him, I let him have it with this blowgun." He seemed very satisfied with his plan and looked to see Papa's reaction.

"Now, let's get this straight, Stewart," Papa said. "We're going stalking, not hunting. We'd like to have you with us, but you'll have to leave the blowgun here. Where'd you get that thing, anyway?"

"I whipped it up this afternoon," said Stewart, twirling it. "It's deadly."

"It's wonderful, Stewart," said Elisabeth, "but we don't want to hurt the bird. We just want to see it."

"Humph!" Stewart muttered, but he left the gun on the porch steps and followed Papa and Elisabeth across the garden, tripping every once in a while over his untied shoelaces.

As they walked down the lane toward the marsh, a very loud sound—a bit like an old automobile horn—made them look up.

"Geese," said Papa. "Look at them!"

Against the sky, now rosy with the last rays of the sun, the dark geese flew in V-shaped groups, their necks straight out in front of them.

"Where are they going?" Elisabeth asked. "So many of them, all at once?"

"They're Canadian geese," said Papa, "and they're on their way back north, after spending the winter in the South."

"They're migrating," said Stewart. Elisabeth looked puzzled.

"That means," said Papa, "that they are moving their homes from one place to another. They fly up to the North and build their nests and raise their babies, and then they fly south again in the fall. The really exciting thing is that the geese, like so many other birds, migrate every year of their lives at exactly the same time and always travel the very same flyway—that's a sort of bird highway."

"Those geese," said Stewart as they continued walking toward the marsh, "are called *Branta canadensis*. And those," he said, pointing to the black ducks swimming along the edge of the millpond, "are *Anas rubripes*." The baby swans, now tired of swimming, were having a ride on their mother's back. "*Cygnus olor*, the mute swan," said Stewart.

"Oh, Stewart, you are so clever!" said Elisabeth. "Papa, isn't Stewart clever! What did he say?"

"Oh, he's clever all right," said Papa, but without much enthusiasm. "He's giving the Latin names for the birds. All birds have scientific Latin names as well as the common names we know them by."

"That must come in handy if they migrate someplace where people speak Latin," Elisabeth said. Stewart growled with disgust.

They turned away from the millpond and crossed the road into the marsh meadow, where the grasses grew tall and the earth was spongy underfoot. As they neared the marsh, the reeds got thicker and the ground wetter. Then the bugle call suddenly sounded.

"That's him!" cried Elisabeth.

Papa said, "By gum, he does sound like . . ."

"Papa!" warned Elisabeth, looking sideways at Stewart.

But Stewart was busy sniffing the air and looking as alert as a bird dog. "He's way back in the northeast quadrant of the marsh," he said.

"This sounds like wet work," Papa said. "But

wait! Stand quietly and look at something else for a minute. See those reeds right over there? Keep your eyes on them."

Suddenly, before their eyes, one of the reeds flew into the air, fluttered a little way into the marsh, and then dropped down among some tall grasses.

"I didn't know plants could fly!" cried Elisabeth with surprise.

"Idiot!" remarked Stewart disdainfully. "Don't you know a bird when you see one?"

Papa laughed. "That's a wading bird, the American bittern."

"*Botaurus lentiginosus*," said Stewart in Latin.

Papa ignored the interruption. "He's a member of the heron family and is very shy. He hides, just as you saw, by pretending to be a reed. He stretches himself up tall, pokes his long beak up in the air among the grasses, and his streaky brown feathers make him almost invisible. People call him the 'stake driver' because his call sounds so much like someone driving a stake into the mud. He goes *oong-ka-choonk*, *oong-ka-choonk*, over and over again."

"I've heard him," said Elisabeth, nodding her head. "Only, I always thought it was somebody hammering on something that never got finished."

Just then the bugle sounded again, and this time it was closer.

"We really need a blind for this kind of work," said Stewart. And then he explained to Elisabeth, "That means we need someplace to hide so that the bird doesn't see *us* but we can see *him*. Maybe we should all climb a tree."

Papa looked about for a good place. "In this

case, I tend to agree with you, Stewart. This ground is awfully wet to sit on, or even stand on, for long." With that, he lifted Elisabeth to the low limb of a willow tree, where she was nearly hidden by its weeping branches just starting to bud. Stewart climbed to a higher limb, and Papa settled himself on a branch near Elisabeth.

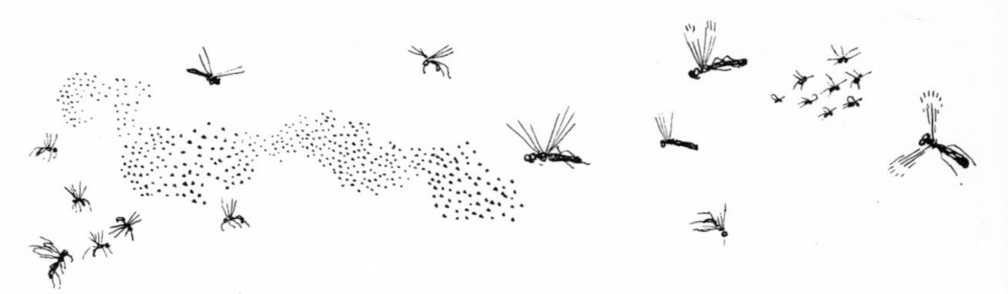

They sat quietly for what seemed like a long time, with dragonflies dancing about their heads. Then Elisabeth whispered, "Papa, in a sort of way it's terribly quiet here, isn't it? But in another sort of way, there's an awful lot of noise in this marsh." And it was true.

At first the noise seemed to be mostly from Stewart's slapping at gnats. But then, through the dusk of the marsh, held close around by the new leaves of trees and fresh marsh grasses, came the sounds of frogs and toads, throaty and watery. The swamp sparrow sang, a horned grebe was going *cow-cow-cow-cowk*, and the red-winged blackbirds were scolding one another. Across the marsh meadow came the lovely sound of the song sparrow, and overhead a gull screamed. In the background the bittern pumped away, and every once in a while there was the bugle call of the escaped exotic.

Then Elisabeth saw something strange, and she poked Papa and whispered, "Look, there's someone else watching from that tree over there. It looks like a very small old man."

Papa looked over at the tree. A hunched figure, in what looked like a gray-and-black business suit, was crouched on a limb just as they were. Papa laughed. "You're looking at the back of a black-crowned night heron. He has his head drawn way down into his shoulders. All herons can fold their necks like that. He should be getting up pretty soon to hunt for his dinner. These herons do most of their fishing in the evening."

Just then the bugle sounded again, and there was a sudden splash. The night heron unbent his legs, unfolded his neck, and, giving a loud *guark*, flew off over the marsh.

The splash was Stewart. He had fallen out of the tree into the shallow water. "I guess I dozed off," he said sleepily. "Gosh, that sound was close!"

Papa climbed down from the tree and pulled Stewart out of the muddy water. He was lifting Elisabeth down from her branch just as Mr. Thew arrived.

"Hello, everybody," he said. "Quite a stalking party! Now tell me all over again about this matter."

Everybody talked at once, and finally Mr. Thew tapped his forehead and looked thoughtful. "Well, let's creep along here quietly and see what we can see," he decided.

When they had gone just a little way along the edge of the marsh, Mr. Thew held up his hand and put a finger to his lips. "The great blue heron," he said, pointing.

There, just ahead of them, standing as still as

a statue, was a big grayish-blue bird on stilt-like legs. His neck was a long, graceful S-shape, and he stared straight ahead as if daydreaming.

"*Ardea herodias*," said Stewart in Latin.

Mr. Thew raised his eyebrows in admiration. Then he said to Papa, "You don't think this could be the monster, do you?"

"From the description the ladies gave us, it could be," said Papa, "but after hearing the exotic's voice, I know it isn't."

"He looks as though he were doing nothing at all, doesn't he?" said Mr. Thew. "But really he's fishing."

Suddenly the statue moved. His long neck darted out quickly, and he grabbed something from the water with his pointed bill. After a few minutes of fishing, he spread his enormous wings and flew across the marsh with his neck folded and his legs trailing.

Just then the bugle sounded quite close. Mr. Thew looked surprised. "My word!" he said. "Let's get down low."

They lay very still in the deep grasses, looking toward a clearing in the meadow. The little insects and the muddy ground bothered Elisabeth, but the suspense was even harder to bear.

A chicken-like gray bird known as a rail came skittering out of the marsh, calling *kek-kek-kek-kek.* The tiniest of herons, the least bittern, was calling *coo-coo-coo* in the marsh grass. Elisabeth wanted to tell them to hush.

Then, suddenly, right in front of them, the bugle call sounded loud and clear. And then they saw the most extraordinary thing! Right there at the edge of the marsh an enormous gray bird began dancing. *Dancing!*

He leaped high in the clearing, then turned and bowed to an imaginary partner. He leaped again, turned, bowed; leaped, turned, bowed. Then he gave one of his loud bugle calls and leaped again; a few small dancing steps, a turn, a bow, a leap, a bugle call.

Elisabeth, Stewart, Papa, and Mr. Thew watched, their eyes wide with amazement.

"A rare sight!" whispered Mr. Thew.

Quite suddenly the bird stopped dancing, stepped into the water, and started to look for fish and frogs. He walked slowly out of sight.

"I don't believe it!" said Papa.

"In all my life," said Elisabeth, "I never saw a bird dancing."

"And for a good reason," said Mr. Thew. "This bird, as far as I know, is scarcely ever, if *ever*, seen in this part of the country. He belongs way out West."

"But what *is* it?" asked Elisabeth.

"A sandhill crane," said Mr. Thew. "A *sandhill crane!* I don't believe it myself."

"What's its Latin name, Stewart?" asked Elisabeth.

"I regret," said Stewart with dignity, "that I am a specialist in only local birds. This crane doesn't live around here."

"It certainly doesn't," said Papa. "And that's why, even when I saw his picture in the bird book, I didn't give him a second thought. Besides, you'll remember that neither Mrs. Peebles nor Mrs. Munch mentioned its most special marking."

"His bright-red forehead!" said Elisabeth. "No one said a word about it. All they said was how big he was. But how did he get here?"

"My guess," said Mr. Thew, "is that he got lost." He picked up a stick and drew an outline on the ground. "Look, this is a rough drawing of the United States. Now, there are four important flyways where birds migrate. See, like this —one on each coast and two up the middle. But the flyways cross each other in some places.

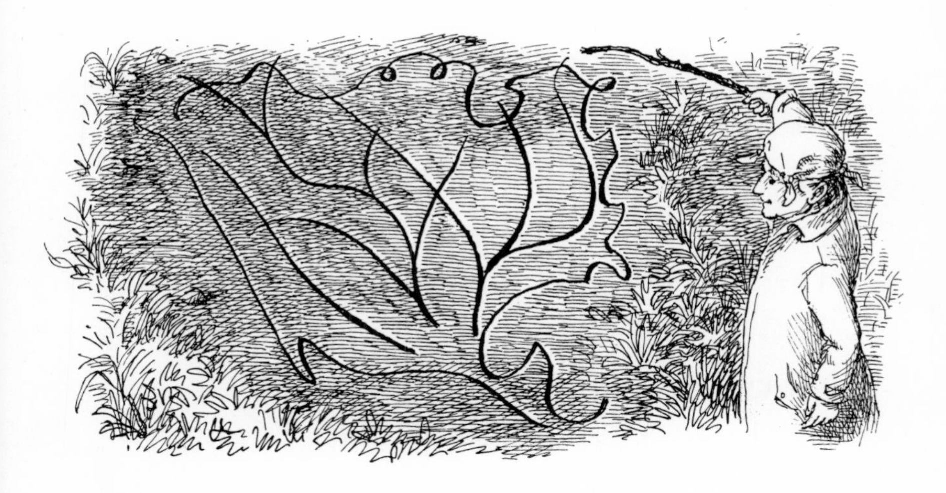

This crane is probably a young first-year bird who may have gotten a little mixed up at the crossroads and, perhaps, joined up with a flight of geese who were coming this way."

"The geese we saw before?" asked Elisabeth.

"Some of those, perhaps," agreed Papa.

"But now he's all alone," cried Elisabeth. "All his family and the other sandhill cranes are somewhere else. What can he do? Can he ever find them?"

Mr. Thew looked thoughtful. "You see, sandhill cranes all migrate along these middle flyways. That's a long way from here. Mmmmm. Now, let's think."

"While we're thinking," said Papa, "let's each have a drink of this hot cocoa." He reached into his pocket for the thermos, some paper cups, and a small package of something that turned out to be marshmallows.

"Keen!" said Stewart.

Everyone squatted down on a fairly dry spot and thought hard. Elisabeth said, "I just love to

have something to have hot cocoa about—like getting frozen sledding or . . ." She stopped to let a sip of cocoa slide hotly down her throat.

"Falling through the ice," suggested Stewart.

"Or just being very, very cold on a very nice day," added Elisabeth, and she popped another marshmallow into her cocoa and let it melt.

While they sat there the moon came up, and the sounds of the marsh sounded stranger than ever in the night. Elisabeth and Stewart started to get sleepy, but Papa and Mr. Thew went on talking quietly. Suddenly Mr. Thew said, "Aha! That's it!" and jumped up and went off toward the road.

"Where's he going?" Elisabeth asked, coming awake suddenly.

"He's got a few useful things in the museum truck that he left parked out on the lane. I'll let him show you what he has in mind himself."

Mr. Thew was back in a few minutes with an assortment of tools on his back and what looked like a hammock under his arm. Then, by the light of the moon and the flashlights held by Elisabeth and Stewart, Papa and Mr. Thew began to put together a very strange contraption.

Right on the edge of the marsh meadow, where they had last seen the sandhill crane, they dug a rather deep hole, which gathered a bit of water at the bottom because of the damp ground. Then they laid the hammock-looking thing across the hole and attached it by ropes to two nearby trees.

When Elisabeth heard that it was called a snare, she was worried. "You won't hurt him," she begged.

"Not a bit," said Mr. Thew. "You see, when the bird steps on it, the net will sink into the hole with the crane right on it. Meanwhile, these ropes will close the top of the net like a bag. Then we'll handle him very carefully."

"Well, that's all right, then, I guess," said Elisabeth. "But when we have him, what will we do with him?"

"I'll tell you *that* when we get him," said Mr. Thew mysteriously.

"Now, all we have to do is wait," Papa said, just as a voice across the meadow called, "Stewart! Time for bed!"

"Time for you, too," Papa said to Elisabeth. "We won't catch this creature until he gets up in the morning, so you won't miss a thing."

"I'll come by for you in the museum truck first thing in the morning," Mr. Thew said. "Good night all."

"Good night," they called to Mr. Thew as they walked back through the meadow in the moonlight.

Elisabeth lay in bed trying to sleep. She was tired, but an assortment of marsh birds kept crossing her mind, picking up their long legs daintily and flapping their wings in a way that kept her awake. Papa was having no such trouble. He had decided to call it a day and had fallen asleep at the count of one.

Suddenly, through the night, a long loud cry made Elisabeth sit up as if she were attached to a spring. "We've got him!" she exclaimed, and she ran in to awaken Papa.

"It can't be morning yet," he complained.

"We must have caught the exotic!" Elisabeth cried, pulling Papa's covers off. "Hurry up!" The cry came again.

With boots hastily pulled over slippers, and overcoats thrown on, Elisabeth and Papa hurried down the lane and into the night, their flashlights laying down a bright golden path for them to walk on. Mama called after them with anxious words like "careful" and "don't."

When they got to the edge of the marsh, where the snare was, something was thrashing about wildly, letting out strange cries. "Stand back," Papa warned Elisabeth, and he shone the flashlight down into the snare. Then he shouted, "Stewart! What are you doing down there?"

For there, in the glow of the flashlight, was Stewart Peebles, very securely caught in the snare.

Elisabeth laughed, and then she said, "Excuse me, Stewart, but you do look kind of funny. What *is* that you're wearing?"

"It's a bird costume," said Stewart. "I thought I could be a decoy and attract the sandhill crane to the snare. But I tripped while I was doing the dance and fell in myself. Hey! Get me out of here!"

Papa pulled Stewart out and untangled him from the snare. He was a very strange bird, indeed, with an Indian feather headdress, which was on crooked, and two kites tied to his arms for wings.

Papa didn't say much to Stewart while he repaired the snare, not even when Stewart suggested better ways of fixing it.

When the snare was all set again, Elisabeth and Papa went back up the lane to the house with its welcome light shining through the night. Stewart slunk off to his own house, dragging his bent wings behind him.

It was very early and still dark when Papa awakened Elisabeth. "Get dressed warmly," he said. "I'll meet you in the kitchen."

In the kitchen, Mama was floating about like a sleepwalker, talking in whispers so as not to wake herself up. She put a dish of oatmeal in front of Elisabeth. "Don't forget your boots," she whispered, and she floated back up to bed.

Just as Papa and Elisabeth stepped out onto the dark and dewy lawn, Mr. Thew drove up in the museum truck. There was an enormous wooden crate on the back of it. "Hop in!" he said.

"Let's stop for Stewart," said Elisabeth. "He won't want to miss it."

It wasn't even necessary to ring the bell at Peebles'. Stewart was waiting at his bedroom window, and before anyone could protest, he had swung himself out on a rope and dropped into the back of the truck with the crate. Mr. Thew drove on down the lane and parked the truck as close to the marsh as he could get. Then they walked across the meadow.

The stars were still in the sky, but the song sparrows were up and singing their lyrical song —*sweet*, *sweet*, *sweet*—and the swamp sparrows accompanied them with trills. The short-eared owl, which flies by day, was sneezing *kee-you*, and the bittern was pumping *oong-ka-choonk*. The red-winged blackbirds, which could be seen in bright flashes as day broke through, were singing *kink-la-reeee*, rising to brilliant, high, quavering notes.

The long grasses brushed them wetly as they approached the edge of the marsh, where the snare was set. The ground grew wetter and made a very pleasing squashy sound under their boots.

Mr. Thew, who was leading the way, suddenly held up his hand.

They all stood still in suspenseful silence for a moment, then Mr. Thew walked to the snare. He waved his arm, signaling them to come closer.

And there he was! The sandhill crane—

quiet now and probably puzzled—wrapped like a gift in netting.

"The *exotic!*" gasped Elisabeth.

"Gosh!" was all Stewart seemed able to say, and he said it several times.

Mr. Thew just gave a kind of sucked-in whistle, and all Papa did was shake his head.

Then Elisabeth said, "But the thing is, now that we have him, what *are* we going to do with him?"

"Aha!" said Papa. "I think perhaps Mr. Thew will tell you about that now."

"Well, here's the story," said Mr. Thew as he started untying the ropes from the trees. "We all know sandhill cranes just don't belong around here. Right?"

"Right!" Elisabeth and Stewart said at once.

"Now, since birds migrate on a pretty good timetable, like the trains, you can tell where they'll be around a certain time of year. It just happens we know that a very large flock of sandhill cranes is due at this time at a big reservation in Indiana. What we think is that we just might be able to—"

Elisabeth cried, "Do you mean you are going to drive this sandhill crane back to his family in Indiana?"

"Not drive," said Papa. "*Fly.*"

"But he doesn't know the way," complained Elisabeth. "That's how he happened to be here in the first place. You said so yourself. He lost his way on the flyway."

"But," said Papa, helping Mr. Thew with the ropes, "we are going to put him on an airplane that does know the way. It will set him down right near the reservation so that he can join the rest of the cranes."

Then Elisabeth looked happy, and Stewart

said, "I would like to say, gentlemen, that you have shown considerable ingenuity."

Papa smiled at Stewart and said, "Thank you, Stewart. That's a very nice compliment, coming from one of your ingenuity."

Mr. Thew cut a long pole from a sapling, and he and Papa arranged it so that they could carry the sandhill crane in its net to the truck. There they set him gently in the crate, loosened the net, and put the top on the crate.

Stewart was dropped off at his house. He couldn't go with them to the airport because of a previous appointment. But Papa, Elisabeth, Mr. Thew, and the sandhill crane rode into the city and out to the airport.

It took a long time and a lot of words to explain everything and work things out with the airline people. But finally it was arranged, and the great plane took off in a *whoosh*—almost, Elisabeth thought, like a heron in the marsh.

When they got back home it was late. A pink dusk had settled on the garden and the house when Elisabeth dropped tiredly, but happily, into the big chair in Papa's study. It seemed a long, long time since she had sat in this chair looking at the bird book with Papa. But it was just yesterday, at this same time of day.

Papa sat down, too, and put his head back and sighed. Then, suddenly, he sat up very straight.

"Oh! Not again!" he exclaimed.

"What is it, Papa?" Elisabeth asked.

"Listen!" Papa commanded. "Just listen to that! It's *another* exotic."

Elisabeth closed her eyes tight and listened for a moment. Sure enough, an unmistakable sound was carried on the evening breeze, across the marsh and the meadow, and into the house.

Then Elisabeth laughed. "Oh, Papa, *that's*

Stewart! That's what he had to do today—have the braces taken off his teeth. *Now* he can play the bugle. Isn't that wonderful!"

Papa wrinkled up his forehead in what started to be a frown. Then he looked at Elisabeth and laughed instead. "Wonderful!" he said.

ACKNOWLEDGMENTS

My thanks to Margaret Stuart, who first heard the "exotic," for all kinds of help in tracking it down.

Roger Tory Peterson's *A Field Guide to the Birds* was used to verify bird descriptions and calls.

Being a
Map of the Mystery –
Marsh,
the Meadow, the Millpond & Mill &
much much more
Drawn by Erik Blegvad
1966
Road to the Airport
Stewart Peeble's
House
Mrs. Munch's
House
Road to the
Dentist's
The Lane
Elisabeth's
House

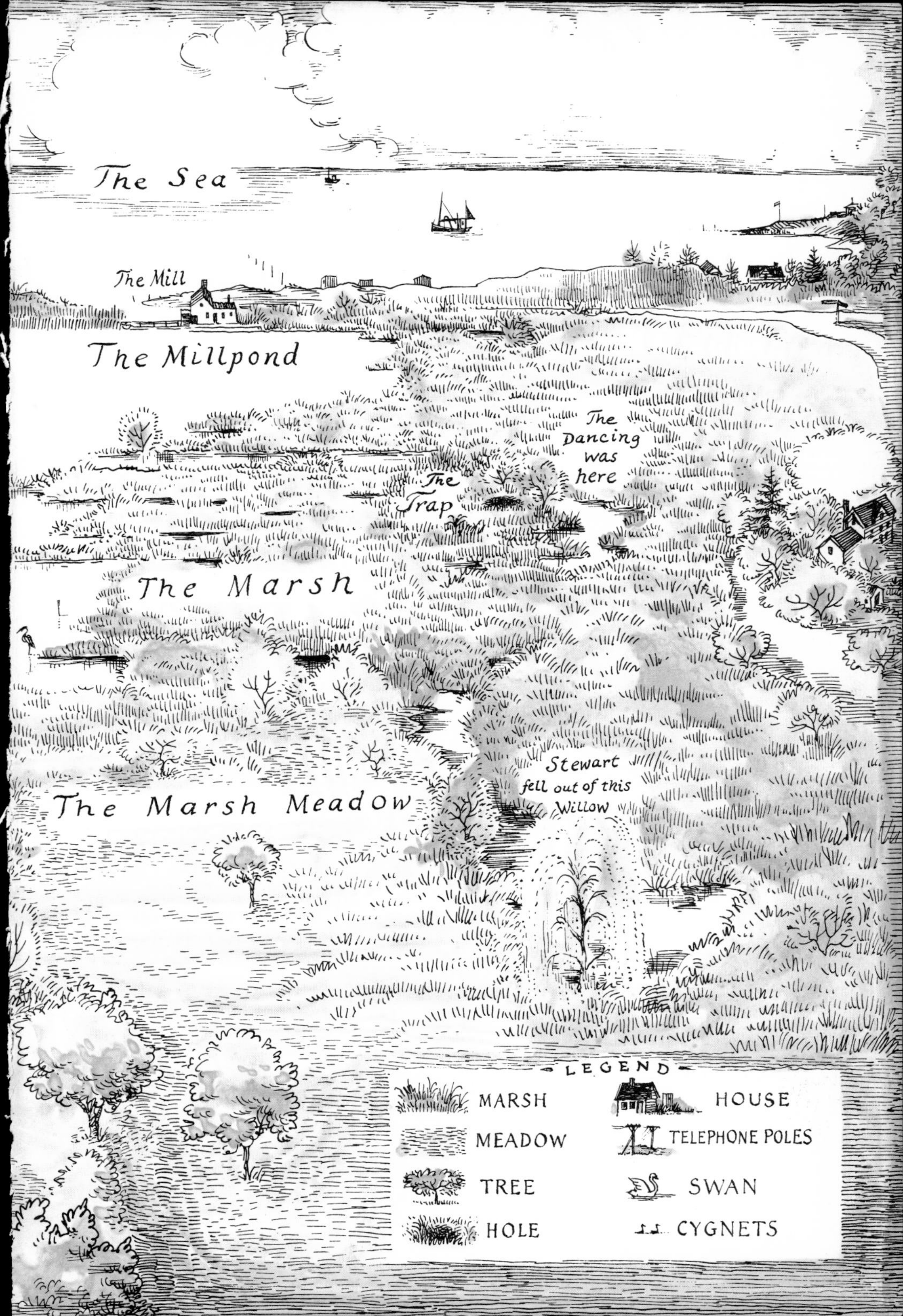

The Sea

The Mill

The Millpond

The Dancing was here

The Trap

The Marsh

Stewart fell out of this Willow

The Marsh Meadow

LEGEND

MARSH

HOUSE

MEADOW

TELEPHONE POLES

TREE

SWAN

HOLE

CYGNETS

DATE DUE	BORROWER'S NAME	ROOM NUMBER
MAR 17	M. matthews	1

Holman, Felice
AUTHOR

Elisabeth and the Marsh Mystery
TITLE

DATE LOANED	BORROWER'S NAME
11-15	D. Quinn
11-22	D. Quinn
MAY 29	D. Pittner
1/9	[illegible]

Strange sounds from the marsh lead Elisabeth, Mr. Thew of the wildlife museum, her Papa, and her friend Stewart to an absorbing investigation.